PRINCESS HEART

Princess Stella Gets SAD

by Molly Martin

pictures by Mélanie Florian

PICTURE WINDOW BOOKS
a capstone imprint

I'm Princess Stella Star Sunny LaMoon.
My castle is quiet and gloomy.

Why?

Because I am sad. And sad is a quiet, gloomy feeling.

Lots of things make me sad.

When I get a bad grade at school.

When my friends won't play with me.

When I lose a game of checkers.

When I feel sick and my tummy aches
and my head hurts.

Today I feel sad because my mother and father left for vacation.

When I feel sad,
I don't want to talk.
I don't want to eat.

I don't want to play.

When I feel sad,
I just want to be alone.
I want to cry. I want to pout.

I know it's okay to feel sad.
A true princess is not happy
all the time.

But a true princess is not sad
all the time, either.

Feeling sad is part of growing up.
There are many sad things
in the world.

But there are many happy
things, too.

When I feel sad, I try to remember the happy things. I talk to someone about my feelings.

Then my sad feelings start to melt away.
My smile returns and everything looks better.

I'm Princess Stella Star Sunny LaMoon,
and my castle is bright and cheerful.

Why?

Because I am bright and cheerful!

Princess Heart books are published by Picture Window Books
A Capstone Imprint
1710 Roe Crest Drive
North Mankato, Minnesota 56003
www.capstonepub.com

Library of Congress Cataloging-in-Publication Data
Martin, Molly, 1979-
Princess Stella gets sad / by Molly Martin ; illustrated by Melanie Florian.
p. cm. -- (Princess heart)
Summary: Princess Stella is often sad, but she has learned how
a princess can cheer herself up.
ISBN 978-1-4048-7853-2 (library binding) -- ISBN 978-1-4048-8109-9 (paper over board)
1. Sadness--Juvenile fiction. 2. Emotions--Juvenile fiction. 3. Princesses--Juvenile
fiction. [1. Sadness--Fiction. 2. Emotions--Fiction. 3. Princesses--Fiction.]
I. Florian, Melanie, ill. II. Title.

PZ7.M364128Prs 2013
813.6--dc23

2012026430

Image credits: Shutterstock/Pushkin (cover background)
Shutterstock/Kalenik Hanna (end sheets pattern)

Printed in the United States of America in Brainerd, Minnesota.
092012   006938BANGS13

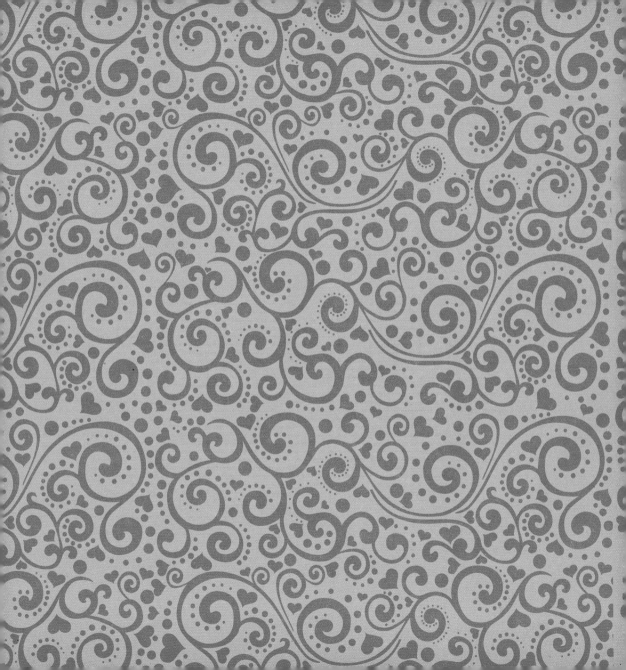